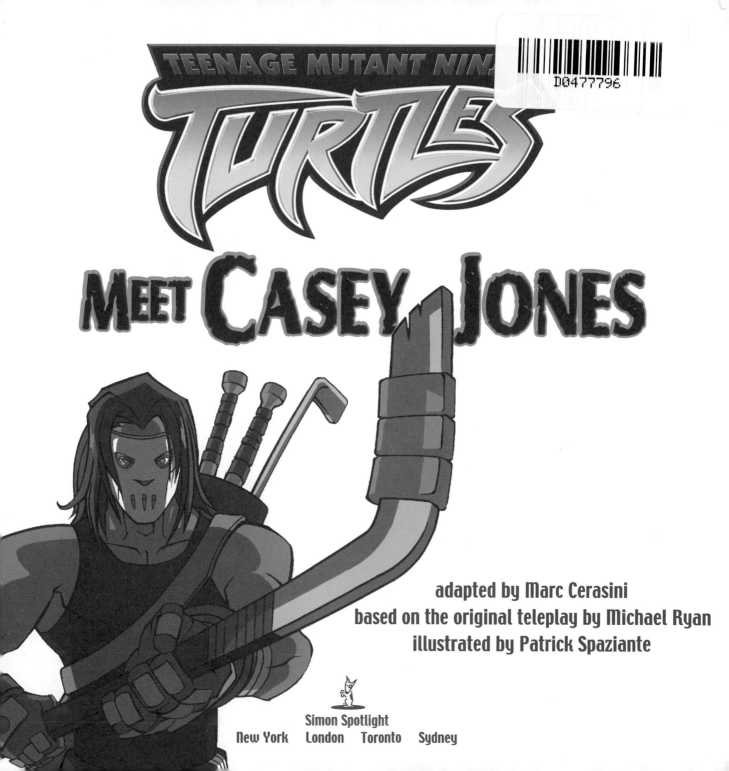

TEENAGE MUTANT NINJA TURTLES

MEET CASEY JONES

adapted by Marc Cerasini
based on the original teleplay by Michael Ryan
illustrated by Patrick Spaziante

Simon Spotlight
New York London Toronto Sydney

SIMON SPOTLIGHT

An imprint of Simon & Schuster Children's Publishing Division

1230 Avenue of the Americas, New York, New York 10020

© 2004 Mirage Studios, Inc. *Teenage Mutant Ninja Turtles*™ is a trademark of Mirage Studios, Inc. All rights reserved.

SIMON SPOTLIGHT and colophon are registered trademarks of Simon & Schuster.

All rights reserved, including the right of reproduction in whole or in part in any form.

Manufactured in the United States of America

First Edition   10 9 8 7 6 5 4 3 2 1

ISBN 0-689-86899-5

In their secret underground lair the Teenage Mutant Ninja
Turtles practiced their ninja skills.

Raphael and Michelangelo squared off for a friendly battle.
Suddenly Raphael charged!

"Ha!" cried Michelangelo, flipping Raphael over his shoulder.

"Nice fall, bro," said Michelangelo.

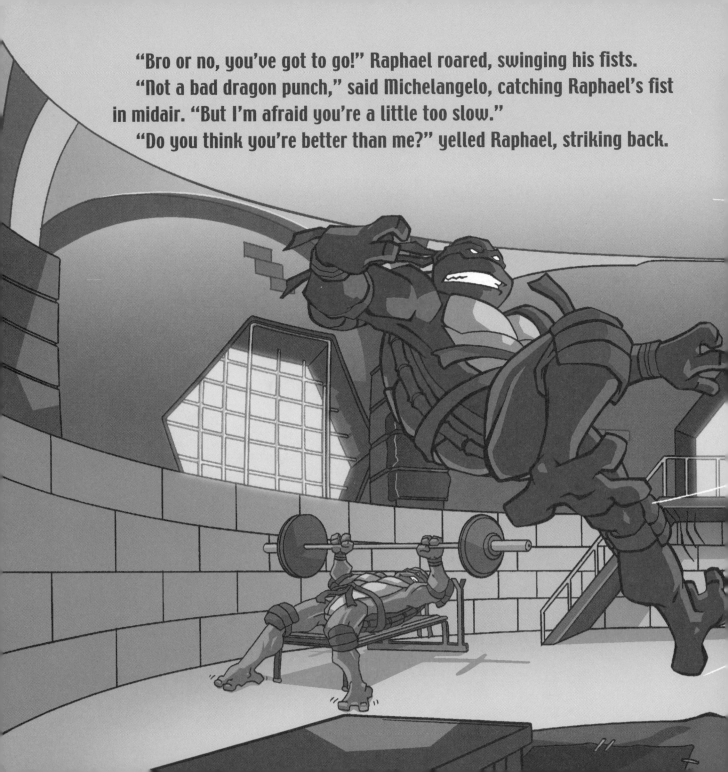

"Bro or no, you've got to go!" Raphael roared, swinging his fists.

"Not a bad dragon punch," said Michelangelo, catching Raphael's fist in midair. "But I'm afraid you're a little too slow."

"Do you think you're better than me?" yelled Raphael, striking back.

"I'm not better," Michelangelo said, dodging the blow. "You're just too cocky."

Now spinning out of control, Raphael crashed into a wooden table, smashing it to pieces. The raging Turtle grabbed a leg from the broken table and swung it like a club.

Raphael was ready to swing again. But this time Splinter grabbed his wrist.

"You must remember that anger is a monster that will hurt you from within," advised Splinter. "You must use self-control. Find balance in all things."

Raphael heard his master's words and knew they were true. Suddenly ashamed, he dropped the club and stumbled outside.

High above the city on the roof of an abandoned warehouse Raphael gazed out at the starry night sky. He felt so ashamed for losing his temper that he just wanted to curl up in his shell and never come out again.

Meanwhile in a rundown apartment not too far away there lived the one man who was even more hotheaded than Raphael. His name was Casey Jones.

"The Purple Dragons are still on the rampage," said the television announcer.

Casey Jones had heard enough. He stormed over to his closet and dug out his sports equipment. He slid a hockey mask over his face, put on his gloves, and grabbed a hockey stick.

"Those Purple Dragons will pay for their crimes!" he roared.

"Hand over the purse and we promise not to hurt you,"
snarled a Purple Dragon member. The muggers were about to
snatch the purse from the lady when they heard a strange sound.
"Oh, Purple Draaaaa-gons! Come out to plaaaaay!"
Casey Jones stepped out of the shadows.

"Bring it on!" said Casey as he spun his hockey stick.

The punks charged. One by one Casey took the punks down until the leader was the only one left standing.

"I surrender! Don't hurt me," begged the Purple Dragon. But Casey Jones stood over him and raised his stick.

"I'm putting you punks out of business once and for all!" he cried.

From the rooftop Raphael spotted the action. When he saw Casey Jones attack the muggers Raphael grinned.

"This is gonna be good!" he said.

But then Raphael saw that the hockey-masked man was ready to clobber one of the muggers—*after* the man had given up.

"That guy's out of control!" cried Raphael. "I have to stop him."

Raphael leaped from the rooftop and landed on a dumpster. Then he rushed to Casey Jones and grabbed his wrist to stop the blow.

"Easy there, cowboy!" the Turtle said. "They're down. It's over."

In the confusion the Purple Dragons saw their chance to escape and ran away.

"Let go! They're getting away!" cried the masked man as he broke free.

"Wait!" cried Raphael, chasing Casey Jones, who was chasing the Purple Dragons. Casey caught up with a Purple Dragon and knocked him down. He was ready to clobber the man, but Raphael arrived in time to stop him again.

"I *told* you to cool it pal," said the Ninja Turtle.

"Yeah?" Casey Jones shot back. "Well, I told you to stay out of my way. But since your ears don't work, I'll have to get my point across *another* way!"

"You're doing the right thing," the Turtle said. "But you're going about it all wrong. What if you grab the wrong guy? You could get in trouble."

"You're the one who's in trouble!" yelled Casey. He pulled back his stick and swung, sending the Turtle crashing into a bunch of garbage cans.

"Goal!" cried Casey.

Dazed, Raphael crawled out of the garbage in time to see Casey Jones hop onto the back of a motorcycle.

"And there's more where that came from!" yelled Casey. "If you want a rematch, I'll be in Central Park waiting for you. Bye-bye!"

Raphael stumbled back to the Turtles' secret lair.

"Wow!" said Michelangelo. "What happened to you?"

"It's a long story," said Raphael. "But first I wanted to say I'm sorry for blowing my top."

Michelangelo punched Raphael's shoulder. "Don't sweat it, bro."

Then Raphael told them all about Casey Jones. "We have to go to Central Park right now and stop him before he hurts someone."

"Maybe we should ask Master Splinter first," said Leonardo.

"And have him stop us!" Raphael cried. "No way."

"Ahem," said Splinter, twitching his nose.

"Busted!" sighed Michelangelo.

"It is dangerous for you to walk among the humans," Splinter said, handing Michelangelo a set of keys. "Take the truck!"

Minutes later a strange noise was heard from the inside of an abandoned warehouse. Then a rusty garage door rumbled open. Bright headlights lit up the dark streets.

Finally tires squealed and rubber burned as the new turbo-powered Teenage Mutant Ninja Turtles Battle Wagon burst out of the garage!

"It's Casey Jones!" yelled Raphael, pointing. "Floor it, Don. Keep up with him!"

"You can catch up to him yourself, Raph!" Donatello replied. "I whipped up a little something special for you. Hop in the back and check it out."

Raphael raced to the rear of the Battle Wagon. He gasped in surprise.

"You are *the Turtle,* Don!" he cried.

A moment later the superpowered ShellCycle burst out of the back of the Battle Wagon.

Soon Raphael caught up with Casey Jones. Raphael cut the spokes out of Casey's rear wheel. The cycle flipped over and crashed. Casey made a soft landing in some bushes.

"I can't believe I just got my butt kicked by a frog," he moaned.

"Turtle," said Raphael, correcting him. "Look, I'll be glad to help you stop the Purple Dragons. But you have to use a little self-control."

"No way," said Casey Jones. "When I was a kid they burned down my father's store. So don't tell me how to deal with the Purple Dragons!"

Raphael suddenly remembered Splinter's words.

"But your anger makes you act just like them!" he told Casey Jones. "You must find balance in all things."

"Isn't this nice!" said a sinister voice.

Raphael and Casey Jones found themselves surrounded by the Purple Dragons. Lucky for them, the rest of the Turtles arrived just in time.

"Friends of yours?" asked Casey.

"My brothers," said Raphael.

"I can see the family resemblance!" Casey said with a chuckle.

Just then the Purple Dragons attacked.

"Incoming goons!" warned Donatello.

The fight was on, and it was fast and furious . . . but the Purple Dragons never even had a chance!

In a whirl of fists and kicks the Teenage Mutant Ninja Turtles—with the help of Casey Jones—took the Purple Dragons down.

When it was all over, Raphael turned to Casey Jones. "I'm glad I met you, crazy man."

Casey nodded. "I think I learned something."

Raphael smiled. "You mean balance? Self-control?"

Casey playfully punched Raphael's arm. Raphael punched him back, just a little harder. Soon Casey Jones and Raphael were wrestling on the ground. The other Turtles looked at the brawlers and shook their heads.

"Let me know when you guys are finished," said Michelangelo. "I'm starving."